# STARDUST
## SCHOOL OF
# D☆NCE

## LULU the
## Ballerina Dreamer

LULU'S HOW TO SAY oh-la-la,
oh-so-French BALLET WORDS LIST

adagio a-dah-jee-oh

allegro ah-leg-grow

arabesque arra-besk

assemblé ah-sum-blay

battement tendu bat-mon tun-do

cambré sharm-br

chassé shah-say

demi pointe dem-e-pwant

échappé a-shap-a

échappé sauté a-shap-a saw-tay

fouetté fwee-tey

glissade glee-sard

grand jeté grund ja-tey

pas de chat pah-da-sharr

petit jeté purr-teet ja-tay

pirouette peer-o-wet

port de bras porte de bra

tendu croisé tun-do kwa-say

FIVE
MILE

Five Mile
the publishing division of Regency Media
www.fivemile.com.au

IN MEMORY
OF JOYCE - ZL

First published 2019

Text copyright © Zanni Louise, 2019
Art copyright © Sr. Sánchez, 2019
Design copyright © Five Mile, 2019

NATIONAL LIBRARY OF AUSTRALIA

A catalogue record for this
book is available from the
National Library of Australia

ISBN: 9781760684624 (paperback)
Printed in Australia by Ovato 5 4 3 2

# STARDUST
## SCHOOL OF
# D☆NCE

## LULU the Ballerina Dreamer

### BY ZANNI LOUISE
#### ART BY SR. SÁNCHEZ

FIVE MILE

# CHAPTER ONE

Lulu Lullaby was spinning through the kitchen, a cucumber in each hand.

'La-la-la-laaaa!' she sang as she spun faster, faster, faster, arms outstretched, eyes closed.

*Lulu Lullaby is the best ballerina the world's ever seen! Look at the straightness of her back. And the precision of her pirouettes!*

*SMASH!*

Lulu opened one eye, then the other. Her breath caught in her throat. *Oh no.* Grandma's precious trophy was lying in a million pieces on the kitchen floor.

'Everything okay in there?' called a croaky voice.

'Yes, Grandma,' said Lulu quickly.

But it definitely was not okay. The Prime Minister gave Grandma that trophy for a Wondrous Career in Dance at the Grand Theatre last year. That trophy meant everything to Grandma. Now Lulu and her daydreaming had ruined it.

Tears welled in Lulu's eyes. She used a brush to carefully sweep the broken glass into the dustpan. The glass pieces sounded heavy as they tumbled into the bin.

The floor was clean again. Lulu stuck her feet firmly to the ground as she cut cucumber and broke lettuce into a salad bowl. She buttered bread and cut cheese.

Lulu carried the food on a tray into the living room with her toes perfectly pointed.

Grandma put down her quilting hoop. 'Oh, Lulu. What would I do without you?' she hummed.

Lulu's heart flinched. *You would still have your trophy, if it wasn't for me*, she thought. But she couldn't tell Grandma. Lulu couldn't bear her disappointment.

Grandma stooped over the fire after dinner. Her back was bent like a coat-hanger. She prodded the coals in the fireplace. Then she coughed and coughed, covering her mouth, her eyes wide.

'You sit, Grandma. I'll do that,' said Lulu jumping up.

Grandma was still coughing as she lowered herself into her armchair and stretched her long, thin legs in front of her.

Lulu glanced back as she prodded at the fire. Grandma's coughing seemed to be getting worse.

Lulu fetched a glass of water, and soon Grandma's coughing stopped.

Grandma put down the glass and looked up at Lulu. Her grin was like a sunbeam. They barely needed a fire with Grandma Lullaby in the room. But her sunny smile wasn't enough to make Lulu forget about the broken trophy.

'Oh Lulu, you look so sad! It's okay. Come, let's look at pictures,' said Grandma.

Lulu forced a smile. She didn't want Grandma to worry. With one foot in front of the other, Lulu glided across the living room. She tried to remember the proper French name for this step. Ah, yes. A chassé.

She picked up the leatherbound photo album, and chasséd back to Grandma.

'Come, my darling Lulu,' said Grandma.

Lulu snuggled in close. She breathed in the album's familiar smell of paper and leather. Lulu always loved to dive into Grandma's world as a prima ballerina.

The old album cracked open. There was teenage Grandma. She stood in front of the Opera House in her tutu, hugging a bunch of flowers as big as her.

There was Grandma in a white tutu, leaping across the stage. Lulu knew this leap's name. A grand jeté.

There was Grandma again. This time with her long hair loose in front of a row of ballerinas. One arm was raised and the other stretched behind her. Her back leg was high. Lulu knew the name of this step too.

An arabesque.

'Ah, *Cinderella*,' said Grandma.
'My favourite ballet.'

She let out a long, sad sigh. 'Those
were magical days. Now look at me.

I can't even stoke a fire.'

Grandma closed the album, and closed her eyes. A little frown pulled her mouth down.

Lulu couldn't help thinking about Grandma's broken trophy.  The guilt felt like a lump of hard coal in her tummy.

Lulu stared at the photo on the album's cover. It was Grandma, with a tiara perched in front of her tight grey bun. Her smile lines stretched the whole way around her face. Grandma, the prima ballerina, clutched her glass trophy for a Wondrous Career in Dance.

'I'm so sorry about your trophy, Grandma,' Lulu whispered to the photo. 'How can I ever make it up to you?'

She slipped the album into its place above the piano.

It was then that she knew what she must do. Lulu must earn Grandma a new trophy. Lulu must become a prima ballerina!

It was the only thing that would make that yucky lump of coal in her tummy go away.

# CHAPTER TWO

Lulu pushed open the yellow door of Stardust School of Dance.

Her teacher, Madam Martine, hobbled towards her. Lulu knew Madam Martine couldn't walk properly because she had an accident when she was younger. It meant Madam Martine could no longer dance. It made Lulu feel sad to think about that.

But, like Madam Martine always said, she still danced in her heart, and now she helped young dancers dance in theirs.

'Class doesn't start for half an hour, Lulu,' said Madam Martine. 'Would you like a cocoa while you wait?'

'No. I am here early to practise.'

'To practise? My, you are keen today. What are you practising for, Lulu?'

'I just want to be the best dancer I can be, Madam Martine,' she said.

Madam Martine nodded and grinned her wide smile. 'You know I like to hear that, Lulu.'

Lulu stretched herself out like a rubber band, just like Madam Martine had taught her. She reached for her left toe. Then she reached for her right. Lulu could almost touch her right foot. That meant she was getting better.

Lulu reached forward with her feet wide. Just one more big breath! *Streeeetch!* The pain made Lulu bite her bottom lip. But it was a good pain. Pain meant she was stretching, and stretching meant she was becoming a better dancer.

With her hands on her hips, Lulu did spring points clockwise around the hall. She turned and chasséd in the opposite direction. She imagined she was a famous dancer, gliding under a big chandelier!

In front of the mirror, Lulu practised port de bras, which means 'movement of the arms'. Lulu pressed her shoulders back, made her back long, with her arms drifting like feathers on a breeze.

'Looking good, Lulu,' Madam Martine called from across the hall. 'I love your passion and dedication ... and those smooth arm movements!' Madam Martine sipped the cocoa she'd made for herself.

Lulu practised so much that by the time the other dancers arrived her cheeks were burning red.

'Hi, Lulu!' said Edmund. He sprung into the air and clicked his heels. At the same time, he flipped his top hat. It spun and landed perfectly on his head, just as his feet landed on the ground.

Lulu grinned and clapped. She loved Edmund's funny dance moves.

Bertie and Priya danced into the hall together.

Priya had a little blue and white bird on her shoulder.

'Look, Lulu!' said Bertie as the girls ran towards her. 'Priya rescued another animal! This is Crayon, the cockatiel.'

'Why did you call it Crayon?' asked Lulu, looking closely at the little bird.

'I found her with a red crayon in her beak,' said Priya. 'She was limping around the play park yesterday, trying to draw on the slippery dip! Lucky for Crayon, I arrived in the nick of time. Didn't I, Crayon?'

Priya bent her nose to the little bird. Crayon gave it a gentle nip.

Lulu giggled and gazed dreamily across the room. Priya was always finding animals to rescue. Lulu imagined Priya's house was like a jungle. Or a zoo! She wondered whether there was room for a bed in Priya's room. Maybe Priya had to huddle up with her animals at night.

'Lulu! Lulu? Yoo hoo, can I have your attention please?' called Madam Martine.

Lulu blinked. The other three dancers were sitting at Madam Martine's feet. She ran over to join them.

'I have some very good news for you all,' said Madam Martine. 'We will perform *Cinderella* for our end of season performance. Won't the costumes be so fun!

There will be an audition next week to work out who should dance which role and ... '

Lulu missed the rest of what Madam Martine said. She could barely contain her excitement and threw her hand into the air. 'I have some very good news too,' she called out.

'What's that?' asked Madam Martine.

'*Cinderella* is my grandma's favourite ballet! She will be so happy to see it again.' Lulu's words tumbled out of her mouth and her eyes were wide with excitement.

There was one more bit of good news that Lulu didn't share. *Madam Martine will choose me to be Cinderella.* Lulu felt sure of it! Her eyes sparkled just thinking about it. *And if I'm Cinderella, maybe an important person from an important dance academy will see me perform. When they see what a magnificent prima ballerina I am, they will ask me to be part of their academy.*

*And then, very soon after, I will earn a trophy for a Wondrous Career in Dance, just like Grandma.*

But Lulu kept that good news nestled deep in her heart.

# CHAPTER THREE

Lulu swept into the kitchen.

'My darling Lulu,' said Grandma, 'will you give me a hand with the pickling?'

'Of course!' said Lulu. 'But first I have to practise my Cinderella steps. Any tips?'

Lulu showed Grandma her moves in the tiny kitchen. She pointed her foot out in a battement tendu.

Lulu thought battement tendu was a funny-sounding name for a dance move. It meant 'stretched beating' in French. Lulu pointed her foot and tapped the air in front of her.

'When Cinderella tidies her stepmother's house, I think she'd move like this,' said Lulu. She walked on demi pointe around the living room, lifting one arm from time to time to dust a shelf or wipe a bench. Demi pointe was the posh way to say 'tip-toe'.

Grandma laughed. 'That does look like Cinderella. I wish I could remember my exact choreography.

But then I danced Cinderella over fifty years ago!' Grandma shuffled over to Lulu and followed her slowly around the room. Grandma couldn't do demi pointe anymore. But she still walked very elegantly. Her dusting was also excellent.

'And now for the pickles, Lulu! Can you please get the bag of vegetables from the bottom of the fridge? My back is terrible today.'

'Yes, Grandma,' said Lulu. Still on demi pointe, she walked to the fridge. At the fridge, she bent into a forward cambré, which is a fancy way of saying 'forward bend'.

Lulu opened the fridge drawer and pulled out a netted bag of vegetables. Then she did the best grand jeté she could, her legs split high in the air, toes pointed. A zucchini flew out of the bag, and landed on the floor on the opposite side of the kitchen.

'Careful!' said Grandma, laughing. 'I don't want dirt in my pickles.'

Grandma's laugh turned into a deep cough. She shuffled to her chair in the other room.

'The curtains open,' said Lulu to her pretend audience, as she cut a zucchini into long, thin strips.

'Lulu Lullaby steps onto the stage as Cinderella.'

Lulu put down the knife and moved away from the kitchen bench. She moved gracefully into a port de bras and a tendu croisé, with one arm raised and the opposite foot pointed in front of her.

'What is this?' Lulu asked her audience, sounding amazed. 'Is Lulu Lullaby about to attempt a fouetté? Oh, how magnificent!'

By now, she was standing in the middle of the living room, one leg outstretched.

Lulu held a pepper shaker in one hand and an open jar of beans in the other.

This was it.

This was the moment Lulu would attempt her very first fouetté, one of the hardest ballet moves of all.

A fouetté was like a fast pirouette with a whipping leg.

Lulu thought a fouetté would be perfect for Cinderella's ballroom scene.

Lulu would need to practise and practise a fouetté if she wanted to be a prima ballerina!

She spun once, twice, three times.

'Lulu Lullaby! Why are there vegetables all across the floor? My Persian rug – it's covered in beans!'

Lulu opened her eyes and looked at Grandma. It took her a moment to work out where she was. She was so dizzy!

'Lulu, I know you love to dance. But you have to be more careful. We cannot afford to waste food!'

A thin line made its way across Grandma's forehead. Lulu didn't like it – that line, or Grandma being cross with her. Especially when all she was trying to do was be the best dancer in the world.

# CHAPTER FOUR

The next week, Lulu skipped into Stardust School of Dance. Priya and Bertie were already there, playing with Priya's cockatiel, Crayon, and her duckling called Quacky.

'Lulu, don't you think Priya will make an excellent Cinderella?' asked Bertie. 'She already has animals flocking to her, just like Cinderella does!'

Something pinched Lulu's heart. She took a deep breath before speaking.

'Yes, but Cinderella is also very good at dusting. I help Grandma with dusting every Wednesday!'

Lulu twirled into a fouetté, which turned into two crossed legs, and a sore bottom.

'Ow,' said Lulu from the floor, as quietly as she could.

Quacky waddled over, and rubbed his left wing against Lulu.

'Are you okay, Lulu?' asked Priya.

'I'm completely fine,' said Lulu, standing and smoothing her tutu.

'In fact, that was exactly what I meant to do.' But Lulu cheeks were feeling very warm.

'Magnificent dancers!' called Madam Martine, shuffling in with Edmund by her side. 'Today, we audition *Cinderella*! Because there are only a few of you, I thought it might be nice if I play one of the tracks from Sergei Prokofiev's *Cinderella* composition, and you all dance the way your souls tell you to dance. Then I can decide each part.'

Priya nodded.

'I like it, Madam M,' said Bertie.

'So do I, Madam Martine,' said Edmund, doing a perfect fouetté, even though he was wearing tap shoes.

Madam Martine pressed the play button on the old stereo. Music filled the room. The class were ready to audition together.

Priya did lots of little jumps, called sautés. Crayon stayed on her shoulder while Quacky ran about her feet.

Lulu wished she could jump as perfectly as Priya. She hoped Priya would be chosen to be the stepmother, or one of the ugly stepsisters.

Bertie lifted an invisible sword and galloped around the room. She ran into an aerial flip. Bertie was so good at spinning through the air, Lulu decided Bertie had to be the fairy godmother.

Edmund auditioned with more of his perfect fouettés. Lulu tried not to feel jealous. She had been practising fouettés since 6 o'clock that morning, and she could only do three, sometimes four, spins without falling over.

*Edmund would probably be the prince*, she thought.

'Lulu? Are you going to dance?' asked Madam Martine.

It was then Lulu realised she had been rooted to the spot for the whole audition, watching the others.

'I would love to see who you become when you dance, Lulu,' Madam Martine said. 'Close your eyes. Become one with the music.'

Lulu closed one eye, but kept the other open, just in case. There was only one character she could become when she danced, and that was Cinderella.

Cinderella was the main part. That meant Lulu had to be the best dancer in the room.

'Okay, Madam Martine. I am ready,' said Lulu.

She stepped confidently into the centre of the hall. She worked hard to perfectly point each foot with every step, and move as a ballerina should walk. Back straight, chin up, shoulders back. She pretended a string was pulling the top of her head towards the sky and became taller still.

Lulu started her audition. She ran on demi pointe around the hall.

Just like she'd practised. Her feet were a bit thumpy, but Lulu made up for it by dusting gracefully with a pretend cloth.

For the ballroom scene, Lulu thought Cinderella might do the polka, a lively hop-step dance. So she danced the polka from one end of the hall to the other as elegantly as she could.

'Careful, Lulu!' said Bertie, who quickly somersaulted out of Lulu's way so they didn't run into each other.

*How might Cinderella dance down the stairs?* Lulu wondered.

Lulu bent her knees then slid her feet out to the sides on tip-toe, then brought her feet together again. This was called an échappé.

'Madam Martine, do you think I should do an échappé sauté?' asked Lulu, after ten normal échappés. An échappé sauté was an échappé with a little jump.

'Just dance how you feel, Lulu,' said Madam Martine. 'Let the music move through you.'

'Yes, but ... do you think a échappé sauté is suitable?'

Madam Martine's scarlet lips stretched out into a wide smile.

But she didn't answer.

Lulu decided she would do three échappé sautés, just to be sure. She landed with a loud thud and hoped Madam Martine hadn't heard it over the music. Lulu ran like a ballerina, and pretended to lose her slipper. She did a pirouette and finished with an arabesque.

Balancing like that, her back foot in the air and one arm raised, Lulu could feel her heart hammering against her ribs.

Other than the odd heavy thump, Lulu was the best Cinderella ever. *Wouldn't Grandma be proud!*

'Well done, my magnificent dancers!' said Madam Martine, switching off the music. 'That was ... how shall I say? Magnificent! Truly magnificent!'

'I liked your dance,' said Edmund to Lulu, as they sat cross-legged in front of Madam Martine, all still panting.

'Thanks Edmund,' said Lulu, grinning.

'It's hard for me to decide,' said Madam Martine, 'because each one of you could be any character in the performance. But I think Bertie – you will make a wonderful prince.

Your sword work was fascinating! Does that suit you?'

'Sure does, Madam M,' said Bertie, grinning at everyone.

'And Edmund, I know it's not conventional, but would you like to play the stepmother? You are so comical, and I think you could have a lot of fun with that part.'

Edmund chuckled. He looked so pleased that Lulu felt herself smiling too.

'I will ask two ballerinas from my Twinkle Toes class to play the step sisters,' Madam Martine explained. 'Oh, it will be so fun!

Perhaps, Edmund, you could also be the coachman who leads Cinderella's pumpkin to the ball.'

'Madam Martine,' said Edmund, standing. 'I would be honoured.' He bowed a long, slow bow.

'And Lulu, with your wonderful imagination, I think you would make a wonderful ... '

*Cinderella. Cinderella. Cinderella,* Lulu silently whispered to herself. She crossed two fingers on each hand tightly in her lap.

'... fairy godmother,' finished Madam Martine.

*Fairy godmother! No. No. No.*

*That couldn't be right.* Lulu was sure she had misheard.

'... And with all those birds, Priya, you must be our Cinderella,' Madam Martine announced.

Bertie cheered loudly.

'Okay. Bravo, Bright Sparks! And farewell, until our next lesson!'

The other dancers bustled off towards the yellow door. They were happily chatting. But Lulu remained cross-legged, shaking her head. She couldn't be the fairy godmother.

*The fairy godmother is not the main part.*

*No prima ballerina was ever just a fairy godmother.*

*What if the important people from the important dance academy come to watch Stardust's Cinderella performance? They won't even notice me!*

These thoughts made tears prickle in Lulu's eyes. She would never win the trophy for a Wondrous Career in Dance now.

'Is everything all right, Lulu?' asked Madam Martine, kneeling down in front of her.

Lulu shook her head and jumped up. She ran from the dance hall. She didn't bother with demi pointe. She didn't notice if her back was straight or toes properly pointed. She didn't even care if her feet were thumpy. It didn't matter anyway.

# CHAPTER FIVE

Lulu pulled her stool close to the fire, and prodded the coals with the iron.

She was feeling gloomy. She couldn't help brooding over what happened at dance class the day before.

'I said are you going to help me make chicken soup, Lulu?' asked Grandma, padding towards her.

Lulu could smell Grandma's lavender powder as she came close. Grandma liked patting powder on her skin to make it soft.

'No,' said Lulu. 'If that's okay?'

'You know I struggle, Lulu. But if you really don't feel like it, that's okay. It's not easy to miss out on the lead role, my darling.'

Grandma shuffled closer to Lulu and wrapped her in one of her special grandma cuddles. 'Sometimes there are bumps and tumbles in a dancer's life, my darling,' she whispered to Lulu, 'but you must dance on.'

Lulu snuggled in close, hugged in lavender scent, feeling the love of Grandma's words in her cuddle. *Maybe everything will be okay after all*, she thought.

But when Grandma disappeared into the kitchen, Lulu remembered the trophy. Now she wasn't so sure.

She heard her grandma start to cough as she chopped. Lulu slinked into the kitchen. She slid the knife out of Grandma's hand.

'Sit down, Grandma. I'll bring you a drink.'

Grandma's watery eyes followed Lulu around the little kitchen.

Lulu moved slowly between the fridge and the bench. She slapped vegetables on the wooden board, and made long, lazy cuts. She tossed the pieces into a pot.

When Lulu filled the pot, water sloshed down the side, wetting the floor.

'Lulu, what is wrong?' asked Grandma. 'Is it about the part? You are certainly not yourself.'

But it wasn't missing out on the role of Cinderella this time. It was the broken trophy.

'I think I have ... a cold,' lied Lulu, sniffing to make her lie believable.

She grabbed some paper towel and quickly dried the floor.

Grandma shook her head. 'Lulu, I've been meaning to ask you all day. Have you seen my trophy? The one the Prime Minister gave me last year? I cannot find it anywhere. I've looked through the bedrooms, in the living room, in all the cupboards ... Even in the attic! How my back ached, climbing those stairs.'

Lulu stood frozen at the bench, looking into the distance.

This was it. The moment that she should tell Grandma what happened.

In her mind, Lulu could see all those glass pieces scattered on the kitchen floor.

She could also imagine Grandma's disappointment, like a heavy, wet sponge.

'I took it to be polished,' said Lulu, her voice tiny. 'A man who works at the key-cutting place said he could make it look as good as new.'

'You did? That is so thoughtful of you, Lulu! I wonder where you came from sometimes. Such a dear, thoughtful girl. I am so very lucky to have you.'

Grandma slowly lifted out of her chair. She did a gentle chassé across the kitchen floor. Very carefully, Grandma did a pas de chat – 'steps of a cat' – towards Lulu. She kissed Lulu's hair, then walked, toes pointed, back to the kitchen chair to sit down.

The guilt was like a bitter taste of coal in Lulu's mouth. She could feel the shape of the horrible dark lump in her tummy.

*Grandma is so sweet. She deserves better than me*, thought Lulu.

Then Lulu had a wonderful thought. It came to her, just as a tiny bird might flit through the air and land on Cinderella's shoulder.

*If I can't earn a Wondrous Career in Dance trophy, maybe I can buy one. I just need some money. Then I will look in every store in the city until I find a trophy. Just like Grandma's.*

The coal taste faded. Lulu stepped into the centre of the room, did five turns of a fouetté, and stepped neatly back into first position. Grandma applauded, her cheeks like juicy plums under her smiling eyes.

# CHAPTER SIX

'Edmund, I need a job. Do you think your dad will give me a job?' asked Lulu before the start of the next dance class.

'I sometimes hand out flyers for Dad's restaurant,' said Edmund. 'Why don't you help me this afternoon?'

Lulu and Edmund stood in the botanical gardens, each holding a thick wad of flyers.

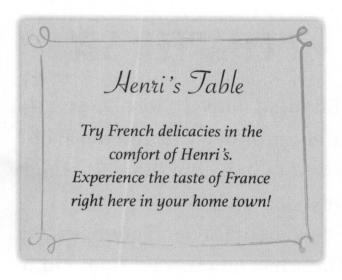

Henri's Table

*Try French delicacies in the comfort of Henri's.*
*Experience the taste of France right here in your home town!*

As people approached, Lulu ran towards them on demi pointe, and handed them a flyer.

'Thank you,' said some people.

'No, thank you,' said others.

One lady with a puffy poodle, and a hat that matched the poodle, was very rude. She sniffed and turned away as Lulu approached.

'Come, Fickle!' the lady said to the dog, pulling it away from Lulu.

The crowds slowed. For a long while, there was no-one to hand flyers to.

Lulu felt worried. Maybe Edmund's dad wouldn't pay her if she didn't hand out enough flyers. She looked around to ask Edmund, but she was too far down the garden path to call out to him.

Lulu distracted herself from her worry by practising a fouetté on the lawn. Lulu tried to do as many perfect turns as she could.

Five turns. Six turns! Her leg whipped fiercely each time. The crowd in her mind applauded.

'Lulu, you should be a prima ballerina, just like your grandma!' said a kind lady in her imagination.

'I should,' said Lulu. She imagined a crowd at the Opera House, clapping frantically. She curtseyed. A deep, proud curtsey.

'Lulu, watch out!' called Edmund.

Lulu opened her eyes.

Flyers scattered across the lawn.
Several floated over the lake and
landed on the surface of the water.

'Oh no!' Lulu scuffled across
the lawn on her hands and knees,
gathering flyers.

Lulu looked down at the flyers she was holding. Some were stained with grass. Some were rubbed in dirt. Others were torn, or folded. She couldn't even think about the flyers that sunk below the surface of the lake. Those were gone.

'I don't think Dad will be happy,' said Edmund, looking unusually serious.

# CHAPTER SEVEN

Edmund was right. His dad was not happy.

Edmund's dad only gave Lulu one dollar, because he said it would cost him twenty dollars to print new flyers. His moustache flicked side to side as he shook his head, as if it was very unhappy with Lulu too.

At the next dance class, Lulu was asking around for a new job. 'Priya, do you know where I can earn good money?' she asked. 'I need a job, and I need one fast.'

'You can help me groom animals at the vet clinic after class,' said Priya. 'Mum is always complaining about dog and cat hair causing her allergies. She pays me in lollies, but I am sure you can ask for cash.'

So after ballet, Lulu went to the vet clinic with Priya. Priya showed Lulu how to gently pull a brush through a German shepherd's long coat. The dog turned to lick Priya's hand. It must feel good to have your fur brushed.

'Like this?' asked Lulu, pulling a fine brush through a tabby's fur. The cat purred.

'Purrr-fect!' said Priya.

Lulu chuckled. She liked grooming the pets while they waited for Priya's mum to make them better. The pet owners were happy their pets were happy, too.

Lulu's favourite pet was Terry, a tiny Yorkshire terrier puppy.

He was so little he could fit into the palm of her hand.

After giving Terry a very light brush, she held the puppy to her chest with both hands and pirouetted through the clinic.

Her pirouettes became fouettés, and before Lulu realised, she was onto her eighth spin! She was getting so good – at last! If only Grandma could see her now.

The imaginary Opera House crowd stood in a standing ovation. 'Bravo, Lulu Lullaby! Bravo!' called the imaginary crowd. A couple of people even threw flowers at her feet.

Something wet fell on Lulu's sleeve, and drizzled down her top.

'Put him down! Put him down!' yelled Terry's owner, a man with a shiny bald head and a thin grey singlet. 'He's sick! Terry is motion sick, thanks to your terrible dancing!'

The man yanked little Terry out of Lulu's arms.

Lulu backed away. She was shocked and very upset.

Priya ran to grab tissues and scrubbed the floor. She also handed a bunch of tissues to Lulu, so she could clean herself.

'You aren't really meant to dance in the clinic, Lulu,' said Priya.

Lulu blinked sadly at the bunch of tissues in her hand.

'... or daydream,' added Priya.

Lulu didn't even say goodbye. She sprinted down the street. She ran away from the angry man and his sick little puppy, and towards Stardust School of Dance. Her eyes were full of tears, so she blinked madly as she ran.

# CHAPTER EIGHT

Lulu was just inside the yellow door, catching her breath.

She could see Madam Martine sitting at her black sewing machine.

*Click-clack-click-clack-click-clack-click-clack.*

The machine sounded like thousands of tiny elves tap-dancing through the hall. Sky-blue fabric burst out of the sewing machine.

It flowed across Madam Martine's lap and onto the floor.

'Lulu!' said Madam Martine, looking up. 'I'm just making costumes for *Cinderella*.'

'I see,' said Lulu. She wiped the back of her hand across her cheeks to make sure Madam Martine couldn't tell she'd been crying.

Madam Martine's round face scrunched as she squinted at Lulu. It was as if she was memorising Lulu, her face was so serious. But Madam Martine didn't say anything. She didn't even offer her cocoa, which was kind of what Lulu

hoped she might do. Instead, she
turned back to the machine.

Madam Martine pushed the
pedal to the floor with her good leg.
The sea of beautiful fabric inched
through the machine, onto the
other side.

*That must be Cinderella's
magnificent ballgown*, thought Lulu
glumly. It looked so lovely that she
could hardly bear to see it.

Lulu walked over to Madam
Martine's old stereo and pressed
play.

The classical music was dark and
slow, just like Lulu's mood.

Lulu moved slowly to the music, while Madam Martine's sewing machine click-clacked away.

Lulu's body felt like water, as she lifted one arm out and stretched her foot. Madam Martine called this 'adagio', which means slow.

The music suddenly changed, and became bright and cheerful ... allegro! It was like sun streaming through a window.

Lulu's body responded. She slid and bounced in a perfect glissade (which means 'glide'), then an assemblé, her feet meeting in the air.

Forgetting Madam Martine was in the hall, Lulu fluttered across the room. She pirouetted. Sautéd. Chasséd! She flew in a grand jeté across the hall. Échappé!

Fouetté! She imagined she was a fairy, dancing through a beautiful garden.

The tiny elf tap dancers stopped. The music lingered.

Madam Martine was clapping. 'I knew you would be a wonderful fairy godmother, Lulu! I just knew it!'

Lulu beamed to hear her dance teacher's praise.

'I don't suppose you would like to put some of that wonderful imagination of yours to use, and help me design the other costumes and the set for our performance?'

Madam Martine asked. 'I have absolutely no idea what we should do!'

Lulu was quiet for a minute, turning over Madam Martine's offer in her head.

Lulu was pretty sure it was her not-so-wonderful imagination's fault that she no longer had a job at the vet. And *that* meant she couldn't get the money for Grandma's new trophy.

And because Lulu could be a bit clumsy and sometimes made thumping sounds when she landed, she couldn't be a prima ballerina.

And that meant she couldn't earn a new trophy for a Wondrous Career in Dance herself. Lulu frowned as she thought about all her disappointments.

Then a happier thought appeared, which made her smile. *But I can still be helpful*, Lulu thought. That was something she *could* do. 'Yes,' she said, finally. 'I will help.'

Madam Martine smiled her wide, red-lipped smile. 'Magnificent.'

'And I have an idea for the fairy godmother's costume,' added Lulu. 'Do you have any fairy lights?'

# CHAPTER NINE

Madam Martine's dance hall hummed with life. It was the night of Stardust's *Cinderella* performance, and friends and family filled the seats that Lulu and the others had set up in rows in front of the stage.

'I really don't know if I can dance in this dress,' said Priya, tugging at Cinderella's blue dress, which hung from a coat-hanger backstage.

'You will be able to,' said Lulu. 'Just imagine you are really at a ball, with a handsome prince, and a real orchestra. You wouldn't be worrying about the dress at all. Dance will pour out of you. You will become Cinderella. That's what happens to me anyway.'

Priya was quiet for a moment. Then her face broke into a smile. 'You're right, Lulu. Just imagining that makes me feel a little better.'

Priya gave Lulu a hug. 'You and your clever imagination. Thanks.'

Lulu smiled and laughed as Crayon bounced on Priya's

shoulder. Priya scratched her feathery chest.

Edmund appeared from the boys changeroom. Instead of his usual top hat, he wore a mop without a handle.

'I love this wig you made me, Lulu!' said Edmund.

'Just one thing,' said Lulu. She chasséd over to rearrange the mop bun on top of Edmund's head. 'There! Perfect!'

Edmund pirouetted in delight.

Lulu peeked out from behind the curtains to see who was out in the audience. The hall was dark.

She could see blobs, which were people's heads. She squinted. It was hard to tell if any of the blobs looked like important people from an important dance academy. But, actually, Lulu realised she didn't care if the important people were there or not.

A spotlight came on at the front of the stage, and Lulu found herself not looking for important academy people.

She was looking for her most important person.

Tonight, Lulu was much more interested in the small lady, draped in a heavy shawl, with long, thin legs stretched in front of her, and a tight grey bun balancing on her head. Grandma sat in the front row, next to Edmund's dad.

*They are probably speaking French*, thought Lulu.

Grandma knew a lot of French, from all her years doing ballet. And Edmund's dad was French.

Grandma's cheeks looked as rosy as Lulu felt inside.

Lulu was very proud of all her hard work.

She had helped Madam Martine string fairy lights across the stage.

She'd painted and cut out a tree for Cinderella to cry under, when she wanted to go to the ball. Lulu had made extra birds and animals, which she'd hung from the rafters.

The spotlight turned off. The hall was dark again. The show was about to begin.

Priya, Edmund and Bertie gave wonderful performances. Lulu was very impressed. The audience clapped in all the right places. And Lulu clapped from the side of the stage, watching them.

Madam Martine told the story through the microphone. But Lulu didn't think she needed to do that. The story told itself through the dance. All you needed was a bit of imagination to work out what was happening.

Lulu's heart fluttered as Priya knelt under the tree and pretended to weep. Crayon rubbed his cheek to hers, to comfort her.

It was time for Lulu to perform. She switched on the lights in her skirt and wings, and stepped out in her flashing costume.

The audience gasped.

'Oh, my! Lulu Lullaby!' she could hear her grandma say.

Lulu couldn't remember the exact steps she had practised. But it didn't matter. Just as she had told Priya, the music crept through her and, with the help of the costume, Lulu did the best allegro dance she'd ever done. She really was

Cinderella's fairy godmother!

The audience clapped. Some stood, in a standing ovation. Lulu bent into a deep, deep curtsey, her heart happy and proud.

But there was one person in the front row, still sitting. Her small back was bent under its thick shawl. Her withered hand covered her mouth. Grandma's rasping cough travelled over the roar of the applause and into Lulu's heart. There was only one thing her heart cared about now. And it had nothing to do with ballet.

# CHAPTER TEN

'I'll take you home, Lulu,' said Madam Martine.

Priya's mum and dad had driven Lulu's grandma to the pharmacy for medicine, then back home.

Because Priya and her sister, Shaan, went with them, there was not enough room in the car for Lulu.

Lulu's fairy lights were still flashing as she walked and Madam Martine hobbled down Blossom Lane towards Lulu's home. Madam Martine squeezed Lulu's hand very tight. It made Lulu feel a tiny bit better. But she still couldn't help worrying about Grandma.

Priya and her family were in the living room when Lulu and Madam Martine arrived at Lulu's house.

Priya's mum smiled when she saw Lulu's flashing fairy costume.

'I hope you've come to grant some wishes,' she said. 'Looks like your gran needed a fairy godmother tonight.'

'Where is Grandma?' asked Lulu, her heart pressing against her chest.

'Your grandma is lying in her room, sweetie,' said Priya's mum. 'I'm sure she'd love to see you.'

Lulu peeked through the gap in Grandma's bedroom door.

Grandma looked like a tiny bird, perched on her giant bed. Her eyes were closed. Her cheeks were pale. The rosiness had drifted away.

Lulu kissed her grandma's forehead. She still smelt like lavender powder at least.

Grandma's eyes flickered. She stared up at Lulu, and smiled.

'Lulu,' she croaked. 'I'm fine. Just fine. The chemist told me to rest, and she gave me some new medicine.'

'Oh, Lulu,' Grandma continued. 'You were so magnificent tonight. Watching your performance was one of the happiest moments of my life. You are such a talented dancer. And so graceful!'

'I'm not graceful, Grandma,' said Lulu. 'I'm clumsy.'

'Come now, Lulu. Don't be hard on yourself! You are elegant, and graceful. A true ballerina!'

'If I wasn't clumsy, I wouldn't have broken your trophy, Grandma.' The words just slipped out. Like a mouse trying not to be seen.

Grandma was quiet.

Lulu could hear Grandma's clock ticking loudly. A bright light buzzed in her bedroom lamp.

'Your trophy wasn't being polished,' said Lulu. 'I know I shouldn't have lied, Grandma. I just didn't want to upset you. I was trying so hard to get you another trophy.' Lulu stared at a loose thread in Grandma's quilt.

'You mean the trophy from the Prime Minister, Lulu? It was glass! It was bound to break. The Prime Minister laughed when I asked if I could swap it for a plastic one, so I didn't break it.' Grandma chuckled.

Lulu noticed for the first time in a long time that Grandma didn't cough when she laughed.

'Oh, Lulu. It was just a trophy,' Grandma continued. Her voice was soft and dreamy. 'The memory though is not made of glass. No, the memory is made of stone, or steel, or ... or gold! Yes, gold cannot break. And neither will my memory of that night at the Grand Theatre, or of my Wondrous Career in Dance!'

The coal of guilt in Lulu's tummy melted away to nothing. Her heart leapt in happiness.

Grandma reached into a little box that sat on her side table. She dropped a little silver ballet slipper on a chain into Lulu's palm.

'For Lulu,' said Grandma. 'Congratulations on the start of a Wondrous Career in Dance. May my coughing never interrupt another performance again!'

Lulu grinned. 'Thank you, Grandma.'

A few nights later, Lulu was sitting on Grandma's lap in front of the toasty-warm fire.

Lulu held the photo album up, so Grandma could see over her shoulder.

There was teenage Grandma, standing in front of the Opera House, still in her tutu, hugging a bouquet as big as her.

There was Grandma, in a white tutu, doing a grand jeté across the stage, under a big chandelier.

There was Grandma, doing an arabesque in front of a row of ballerinas.

Grandma moved around the pictures in the album to make room. Then Lulu stuck in a new photo.

It was a photo that Edmund's dad had taken with his camera the night of her *Cinderella* performance. In the photo, Lulu was dressed as the fairy godmother, and was doing her ninth rotation of a fouetté. The fairy lights in her wings made dappled light across the stage. Her skirt mushroomed out, and glowed like a firefly as she spun.

'Ah, *Cinderella*. My favourite ballet,' said Grandma.

'Mine too,' said Lulu.

**THE END**

# More about the STARDUST dancers

# MADAM MARTINE

Madam Martine has always loved dance. When she was younger, she practised hard for many years and eventually became prima ballerina for the New York Ballet. Sadly, an accident meant Madam Martine could no longer dance. But it was then that she discovered she could always dance in her heart. And that she also loved to teach kids to dance. So she created Stardust School of Dance! Madam Martine loves hot cocoa, swirly dance skirts, and helping her young dancers realise their dreams.

# BERTIE BLACK

Psst. Don't tell anyone, but Bertie Black is secretly a ninja. She keeps a secret ninja diary, and spends her spare time practising her awesome ninja moves. She's an aerial-flip specialist. But Ninja Bertie has recently discovered she also loves to dance. Bertie lives with her step family on Blossom Lane, just across the road from the Stardust School of Dance. She loves climbing trees, animals, perfecting her ninja moves and her new friends. She is part of Stardust's Bright Sparks class, with Priya, Edmund and Lulu.

# LULU LULLABY

Lulu Lullaby lives with her grandma on Blossom Lane. Her grandma was once a famous ballet dancer, and she's taught Lulu everything she knows about ballet. Lulu knows all the fancy French names for ballet steps. As well as dancing, Lulu loves to daydream. She's also a very caring friend and granddaughter. Lulu dreams of being a famous dancer one day, just like her grandma. She is part of Stardust's Bright Sparks class, with Edmund, Priya and Bertie.

# EDMUND FONTAINE

Edmund Fontaine's dad would like Edmund to be a chef, just like him. But Edmund is more interested in dance. Edmund spends rainy Sundays watching his favourite movie, *Singin' in the Rain*, and can perform Gene Kelly's dance routine perfectly. The only time you'll catch Edmund out of his tuxedo and top hat, is when he's wearing his dance clothes. Edmund is a good friend, and an excellent tap dancer! He is part of Stardust's Bright Sparks class, with Lulu, Bertie and Priya.

# PRIYA PATEL

Priya Patel is an animal whisperer. She helps animals who are in trouble or need a friend. She and her sister Shaan have lots of pets at home, but Priya's closest companion is Petit Jeté, her sausage dog. Priya's mum is a vet. When Priya isn't spending her free time at Stardust School of Dance practising her moves and hanging out with her friends, she's most likely at the vet clinic helping her mum. She is part of Stardust's Bright Sparks class, with Bertie, Edmund and Lulu.

# READ MORE STARDUST

HAVE YOU READ BOOK #1?

## BERTIE
### the Ninja Dancer

Bertie Black has just moved in with her new step family, but it doesn't feel like home. She spends her time practising cool ninja moves, until the sound of music carries her to Stardust School of Dance. She is offered a role as a dancing shepherd. But will Bertie take her ninja moves from the shadows to the stage? If she does she might find a real home at Stardust. But will she take the leap?

BERTIE
the Ninja
Dancer

STARDUST
SCHOOL OF
D★NCE
BY ZANNI LOUISE
ART BY SR. SÁNCHEZ